Pain to Fame

Flairs and Glairs
Publication House

Disclaimer

This is a work of fiction and solely represent the thoughts of the corresponding authors of the articles. Our editors have tried their best to edit the content of all the authors and check the plagiarism.

All the write-ups in this book are unique and are only published in this book.

In case any plagiarism or error is found, only the author is responsible alone, and not the publisher or the Compilers.

Cover Designing and Book Formatting
Shubham Shah and Ishani Agarwal

Co Authors

1) Shubham Shah (Founder)
2) Ishani Agarwal (CoFounder and Compiler)
3) Anjana Agarwal
4) Ishika Agarwal
5) Rubal Choudhary
6) Bidyashree Jogajanma
7) Divya Syamala
8) Khushi
9) Grishma Ninave
10) Ishrat jahan Noormohammed khan
11) Jagriti Pramanik
12) Prachi Mayuresh Kunkalienkar
13) Rutuja Gahukar
14) Vaishni Venkatesh
15) Zala Ramiben Devsibhai

Shubham Shah
(Founder)

Shubham Shah, an entrepreneur at "Flairs & Glairs" a brand with dynamics in events organizing and cultural educational pan INDIA, is a 26yrs old guy who recently has entered the digital platform of imprinting emotions. He has initiated with his own open mic platform to help budding poets and aspiring writers under his brand named as "Teekhe Zasbaaat"
He is a commerce graduate from the Bhagalpur City of Bihar. He states Writing has impersonated him since childhood and he has now been writing for over a decade!

Cooking, on the other hand, is his passion! He also mentions, trying out new things just tickles him!

When asked sir, Why SPICY EMOTIONS?

He smiled and added, "agar jasbaat teekhe na ho toh wo jasbaat kahan" Spices are all that blends! So do his words!

As a chef, he presents to you his dish! Hot and freshly served! Taste it! Feel it! Enjoy it! You can also find his writing in the Book "Teekhe Zasbaaat" and 50+ Co-authored anthologies. With his passion to explore opportunities across Platforms, he is working with keen devotion and We wish him all the very best for his future ventures.

He is Featured in the International Magazine DeMode for his upcoming solo novel.

He is Approved by Ne8x for its Lit Fest, and is a Golden Star Awards 2020 Winner.

He is a India Book of Records Holder for his Anthology Satrang, and has the Grandmaster title by Asia Book of Records, for the same.

He has also been featured in Prabhat Khabar, Dainik Jagran, and a lot of other Newspapers in Bihar for his achievements.

He has been a proud co-author to

India Book Of Records (Title- Black)

World Book Of Records (Title -15 Wonders of Poetries)

India Book Of Records (Title - Aaina)

Vajra World Records Holder (Title - Gustakhi Maaf Hai)

High Range of Records Holder (Title - Gustakhi Maaf Hai)

Indian Book of Records

(Title - Road from Worst to Best)

Share your reviews on his

INSTAGRAM

@spicy_emotions
@shubham4shah

Or via email on

shubham2shah@gmail.com

To stay tuned to his work and opportunities follow his business Handles

INSTAGRAM   FACEBOOK   YOUTUBE

@flairsandglairs
@teekhezasbaaat

WEBSITE:

https://flairsandglairs.in/
Https://Flairsandglairs.Com/

Towards The Destination

The journey began as a student planning and plotting every aspect on how the career path should be, but all it turned out was an unforeseen coordinate where life just brought me to.

Towards an unplanned destination, a journey was set up just like a roller coaster without any knowledge of what and how shall things turn out to be. But yes, I can proudly say that there is someone, who is guiding me all through this voyage. I feel like driven cattle who is being asked to head in a direction keeping everything rest assured to be fulfilled with time.

As a teenager who was about to complete his 10th Boards and was asked on what his future are, the only predefined answer was, 12th, followed by a BBA graduation heading to MBA and then a lavish life in corporates.

It would sound like a joke if I say that I also struggled through the entrance of CA, CS and FRM. But I must say it was a training period of life that taught me everything.

But at the end today I stand at a position that is slowly and steadily giving me what I deserve.

"At the end of the day everything falls right into place"

Ishani Agarwal
(CoFounder)
(compiler)

Ishani Agarwal hails from the City of Joy, Kolkata.
She is the co-founder of her Community "Teekhe Zasbaaat"
and Flairs and Glairs Publication.

Been a Compiler for 45+ Anthologies, she is in the process for more. Co-authored in 150+ Anthologies. She is a India Book of Records Holder, a Vajra World Records Holder, a High Range of Records Holder, an OMG Book of Records Holder and a Bravo Record holder.

Approved by Ne8x for its Lit Fest 2020, and Literary Icon 2020. Also a Golden Star Awards Winner 2020.

She has also been awarded with India Star Republic Award 2021, a part of She Awards by Awards Arc and Winner of Nari Samman 2021 by Literoma.

She is also selected as Best Achiever of the Year by AwardsArc and Most Challenging Compiler Award by Spectrum Awards.

She has been featured by the National Magazine "Taree Zameen Par" with the title 'unstoppable'.

Also featured in the International Magazine DeMode for her upcoming solo novel, she is proud to write on social issues, and is happy with the love she is receiving.

Connect with her on Instagram: @Ishani_agarwal_quotes / @compilations_so_far

<u>Her Achievements</u>

1) A+ NCC Certified Cadet
2) Participant of RD Parade Kolkata for a stretch of 2 Years
3) Head Girl of my School
4) Winner of Inter College Business Case Study Competition
5) India Book of Records Holder for her Anthology Aaina
6) Vajra World Records Holder for her Anthology Gustakhi Maaf Hai
7) High Range of Records Holder for her Anthology Gustakhi Maaf Hai
8) Featured in an International Magazine DeMode
9) Golden Star Awards 2020 Winner
10) Nominated by Ne8x for its Lit Fest 2020
11) Co-author of 15+ Record Aimed Anthology
12) Published my Solo Anthology with 750+ Writeups, titled " Hand That Burnt While Healing".
13) Featured in a National Magazine "Taree Zameen Par" in the Column 'Break+ UpSuccess with the tag "unstoppable".
14) Bravo World Records Holder for her Anthology 'Ek Naari Sabpe Bhari' for being the fastest Anthology.
15) Winner of She Awards by Awards Arc
16) Indian Book of Records Holder for her Anthology "Road from Worst to Best".
17) BTC Award Winner
18) OMG book of Records Holder for her Anthology " Your Emotion our Motivation".
19) Nari Samman Awards 2021 winner
20) Awarded India Star Republic Awards 2021.
21) Awarded She Awards by Awards Arc
22) Awarded as Best Achiever of the year by Awards Arc
23) Awarded Most Challenging Compiler Award by Spectrum Awards
24) Forever Star Book of World Records for her achievements.

<u>My Success Story</u>

Life goes on. But how beautiful or worth living your life is, is dependent on you.

My life was plain and average. But then, it changed one day.

My Writing journey started. I never even knew I had the knack for writing, let alone other things. But it turned out, that was a life changer for me.

It was through this journey that I realised what my true worth is, and what gives me pleasure.

Oh, and not to forget, recognition.

A lot of people supported me, became my backbone. While a lot thought it was all worthless. Friends and foes, I met all here. The ones who called you family, but were the first ones to talk behind you, they are the reason I was determined to prove myself.

And my hardwork did start reaping off. Records and Awards paved its way open for me.

Starting from one, to the next, to the next.

Today, I can proudly say that I am a holder of 7 Records (Including both Indian and World), and 10+ Awards from all around.

Yes, my journey took me a year and a Half, but today, one thing I can proudly say -

I am what I am, because of what I did.

When my family looks up at me and says they are proud of me, I feel i have achieved it all.

Anjana Agarwal

I am Anjana Agarwal.
Writing has been my way of expression since i was small. Itz coz writing gives me happiness.
Born n brought up in Shelling, married in Kolkata, its through words that i portray emotions best.
Been a Co-author in 50+ Anthologies in the past 1 yr.
Insta handle: anjana5408

Ishika Agarwal

Ishika Agarwal.
Being a class 12 student, my imagination ran wild. I tried penning down my imaginations.
Love Writing. It is nothing else but a passion.
From Kolkata.
Also, into extracurricular activities!
Appreciated by India Book of Records for my solo Book, "Love – A gift or a curse".
Been a Co-author in 70+ anthologies in the recent past.
Insta handle: ishika_agarwal13

Rubal Choudhary

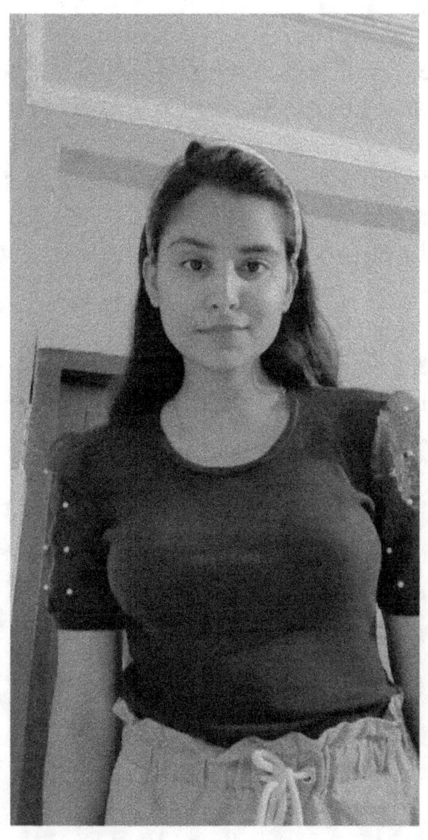

A girl with wings, who not only wants to fly but also wants to achieve all possible things which can be achieved on this planet.
Just like the falcon she wants to fly high, breaking all barriers coming in her way.

Her name is Rubal Choudhary and she is from Gurgaon, Haryana, Currently doing English Hons. from Delhi University.
She aspires to become a Govt officer.
A selenophile, avid read, artist and what not, she is an ambivert and a learner who only wants to learn and grow.

She has compiled 30 books till now and 2 solo books are coming on her way.
She has been honoured with alot awards and 4 National and International Records.

To get in touch with her, you can contact her at rubal.choudhary27@gmail.com

<u>My Journey</u>

Writing was a not a cup of my tea and we have always heard Unexpected things are the most beautiful and yes it holds true in my case.
Writing has given mt the most beautiful thing, "My Growth".

I never thought to write but with time I got interested into content writing and then it all started. Preparing contents for different blogs, websites etc was fun and trust me the best part was to do reasearch.
And I as a person loves to read and search about anything and everything which is possible on this entire planet.

We never know, when will our life take an unexpected turn in the right direction, so it happened with me.
Through content writing, I met few people, and got to about writing.
From writing quotes to posting it on Instagram to connect with people
I explored with time.

Then came a time, where I got to know about Anthology, publishing and etc.

And from there my real journey began.
Firstly, a co-author, then a compiler and finally the Head of a publication house.
Working day and night is what I like and perfection is in my blood.

And, then my fate changed, the only thing I ever dreamt of was being a record holder, I worked day and night, talked to

a lot of people, verified everyone's write up and finally became an "India Book of Record" Holder.

From their my journey to be a successful record holder continued.

I achieved Vajra World Records, Kalam World Records, and the most prestigious and the hardest one, Asia Book of Records.

I then started earning titles, "AAJ KI WOOMANIYA" is my favorite, it actually defines me, "beauty with brains" and a "kiddo with perfection".

From then till now, I have got a lot of recognition from a very renowned places and I am proud of my all the achievements.

It's all about thinking, working and achieving.

Every second person can think but very less have the potential to achieve and I am one of them.

Bidyashree Jogajanma

Bidyashree Jogajanma is from temple city Bhubaneswar ,Odisha. She likes to pendown with emotions and it becomes her passion .She is an Assistant professor(UgcNet qualified) did her master's in Public administration, Sociology, Psychology after Btech(Automobile).She is also a social activist with part time counsellor and Astrologer.

She is also a renowned dancer where she got lot many awards 30+ including South Asian Youth award.

She has been awarded with

 Bharat Ratna Rajiv Gandhi Award for two times.
She is a gold medalist in Race National competition,
She has also been awarded with Baisakhi Award,
Rajyastariya prativa samman, Madan mohan biswa parishad
award, Virat Dhanu Yatra Award, Biswa parishad award and
many more as a best classical dancer.
She got featured in Magazine"Kadambini "
She is the co-author of 10+anthologies in recent past.
She likes to write on social issues through which she wants
create social awareness among people.

How I Will Feel When I Get The Fame!

In this giant Earth, standing in a small piece of my mother land!
Goose bumps on my skin, while hearing my name.
Lots of applauds cleared the image which got blurred,
Those strrugles,determination pays off !
When I had listen to the spark which was obscure .
Failed many times but wipes the dust without wasting my time.
Was the part of prejudice but broke to give justice,
Justice to myself, my dreams, my times!.
Stopping me is impossible i made my everyway possible.
Those sparkles of my eyes tells everything
I feel blissful being recognised even if l lost something.

<u>Its Only About Decision</u>

I make the path towards the success by coming over it,
Got threaten by failures but hardly get convinced by it,
But my dreams persuade me.
Positive action with determination was the key,
Which I endeavour to continue inside me.
Waxine and vanine was part of life,
To taste the sweetness i had walked over the edges of knife.
Lots of pressure was there of being cut down ,
I slipped! i fell ! my laser focus never let me down.
Loads of pebbles throughout my journey,
I shine like marbles by creating opportunities .
Its only about the decision
Should i cry on my luck ?or inspire others ?
But choose to radiate like sun.

Divya Syamala

This is Divya syamala hailing from Vizianagaram, Andhra Pradesh.
She was an introvert person.
To express her feelings she doesn't have many friends. Though it was late she started to find a way to express her thoughts and feelings through her writings.
She started writing from one year even though it's not a cup of tea for her in writing but still trying in her own way in her own aroma. She loves to do new things and likes to travel.
Been a co-author nearly in 10+ anthologies.
Insta handle : divi_syamala

<u>Ways of Recognition</u>

An infant cries to get attention
A baby does gestures for recognition
A girl gets ready to get an applause
A teenager does things to get attract by others
A boy does heroic acts to get identified
A teacher looks angry to get attention of their students
An entrepenuer attracts the salers through his discounts
A business man accredits through his strategies
A leader gets accepted through his leadership qualities
A speecher gets appreciation through his speech
Everyone in this world fight for recognition every day...
Recognition became our part in daily life....

<u>Struggle To Get Recognized</u>

A long time ago there is a village where music was banned. Years were passing nobody dares to sing. However as time goes by a child unknowingly began to sing when he saw the nature. With his voice and the pitch even nature starts chorus.

Not long time someone found he was singing a song and they blamed his family and warned the child not to sing. But the child never gave up. He started to sing where nobody was around.

One fine morning he went to the forest and started to sing. As he was singing he came across the parrot and asked how am I singing but the parrot flew. He was disappointed and started to sing again and moved on. Again he come across a beautiful sunflower and asked how am I singing but the flower goes to wrinkles all of sudden and he was sad and disappointed but he never stopped to sign.

After moving forward he came across a river and make the river to listen his singing and asked it's opinion but the river flows very fastly. He was disappointed and started to cry why everyone was running away from me? He doesn't know why they are avoiding. He started to cry loudly. Then the cloud appears and said don't you know the banishment to sing in your village. He started to think about it and said why to banish to sing and I won't accept this. I will make myself singing in village.

The very next day he took permission from his parents but they didn't agree because they were fear of their village heads. But the child never gets fear and prepared himself alone. He make himself courage and make announcement to gather everyone at the center of the village. Everyone was whispering themselves and the boy took courage and started singing. First they didn't agree but while listening his voice

everyone enjoyed and involved in his singing. They forgotten everything and they immersed in singing. When he stopped they came out of that mesmerized situation and started congratulating him with his singing. He then stated that why should we ban singing without a reason. We are living in a society to do what we wants and what makes us happy but not those unreasonable banishment things.

The child worked hard even though he was cursed, foul mouthed but he never giveup. When you want to be recognised uniquely always have to work hard in your own way even though society not agree. Never step back from your dream. We should not wait for recognition, it comes all the way when you did the work wholeheartedly. Here the child did it and we can do too...

Khushi

Heya!

I'm Khushi,a touchy & moody girl,jolly in nature.Born and raised in Haryana.I'm an amusive & focussed person.Best since 23-10-2003 & a pupil of Grade12.I view myself as a lawyer in future.Some of my hobbies are singing,cooking,sketching and writing.Writing being my best part,always aids me conveying my feelings on a piece of paper.

Being an interactant,will be happy connecting with you on my insta profile @khushiii2003

Thank you!:)

कामयाबी

आसान है क्या कामयाबी पाना
इतनी ऊँची चढ़ाईयाँ, ऐसे हि चढ़ जना
टूटना और फ़िर संभल जाना
आसान है क्या कामयाबी पाना।

मंज़िल कि हासिल ,तो साबशी पाना
ना मिली तो आँखें चुराना
बुरी संगत से ख़ुद को बचाना
आसान है क्या कामयाबी पाना।

बार बार चढ़ना और फ़िर गिर जाना
"तु कर सकता है" हर बार ख़ुद को समझाना
पैसों की किल्लत , भूखे पेट सोना
आसान है क्या कामयाबी को पाना।

कुछ भी हो जाए
बस हार नहीं मानना
गिर जाओ तो ख़ुद को उठाना
अपने आँसुओं को पोंछकर वो हँसी वापिस लाना
आसान है क्या कामयाबी को पाना।

हार नहीं मानूँगी

मैं जितनी बार गिरूँगी
मैं उतनी बार उठूंगी,
ऊँचाइयों का रास्ता
अपने हाथों से बुनउँगी
पर हार नहीं मानूँगी।

मैं रोऊँगी मैं हसूँगी
मैं माथे पर कफ़न क्सूंगी,
मेहनत के दम पर
आगे ही बढूंगी,
पर हार नहीं मानूँगी।

मैं सपने देखूँगी
उन्हें पुरा भी करूँगी,
मैं पीछे कभी नहीं देखूंगी
हर मुश्किल पार कर दिखाऊंगी,
पर हर नहीं मानूँगी।

लोग गिराएँगे
पीछे खीचेंगे,
मैं लोगों की नहीं सुनूँगी
बस अपने मन की करूँगी,
पर हार नहीं मानूँगी।

Grishma Ninave

A student of science and an admirer of arts.
A science graduate cherishing the art of writing, working as a project head at Flairs & Glairs Publication House. Published in the Editorial section of a national magazine as Aaj Ki Womaniyaa, in the first edition of 2021. She has won the Be The Change Award, AIBA Award, She Award, Applause Awards, etc.
A minion millenial with extra-large dreams.
Is in active rebellion with her mother about the number of books she must have in the house.

When not reading, can be found writing and reviewing books a lot.
Firm believer that music is what can revive and reconcile the world.

She's one of those people who love greys more than colours and she's like a colourful autumn too at the same time.
Admires old school love stories and retro music.
A Capricorn girl who believes hearts are more important than physical appearances.
Is into deep talks with a very few people, but believes they are the driving force of joy in her life.
Loves traveling to places where there are mountains, trees, hills and treks.
No wonder nature's beauty strikes a chord within her.
The guiding light in her life is the quote, "Don't search for happiness, because it's not something you find, it's something you create!"

Has participated in around 150 anthologies and compiled many titles too.

<u>Evening</u>

This evening can easily reflect,
What lies within my soul.
Like my smile is bound to reject,
The pain in my eyes, dark as coal...

These raindrops fall in the sea,
To vanish their own existence.
Like my tears wash away the plea,
That the heart makes to the mind's pretence...

As the streetlights light a dark street,
And the soul seems to be tied by a rope.
Highlighted are the wounds on my feet,
By the little pieces of the then shattered hope...

The Moon's loneliness reminds me of my own,
I'm pregnant with anxiety as my baby.
But the way is shines despite the lone,
Makes me think one day I too shall shine, maybe...

<u>Growth</u>

Within me which lies,
Is an aesthetic young girl,
Who still silently defies,
The upcoming youth's whirl.

With feelings and dreams new,
While the meanings of colours change,
Learning to be in other's shoe,
My thoughts I begin to rearrange.

As I spread my wings,
Staring at the sky I await a new dawn,
To me a new hope clings,
And the older orchestrates of belief yawn.

Now I am ready to fly,
Fantasizing of all the claps I will hear,
Looking beyond what's true and what lie,
And pushing behind my enemy called fear.

Ishrat Jahan Noormohammed Khan

Ms Ishrat Jahan Khan holds 15 years of teaching experience as full time Teacher at present she is designated as Asst. Head Mistress for Secondary and Higher Secondary section at St.Anthony's Convent Higher secondary School and project head at Flairs and Glairs and she has 5 years teaching Experience as a part time Teacher

12 years of teaching experience in Coaching Classes

She has Special achievements which are :-

1She has been awarded as best National english and psychology teacher award from the hands of esteemed guest Urmila Mathondkar

2.She received Best Teacher awarded from rotary Club of Ulhasnagar in the 2010.

3.She has an Appreciation Award from SACHSS for HOD,
4.Appreciation certificate from rotary club of Badlapur industrial Area for participating in "Capture the Nature",
5.Appreciation Certificate for Guiding the Students Of interact Club,
6.Award of Appreciation for Organising SPARK event,
7.Appreciation certificate for short film Schizophrenia,
8.Award from ICE English scholarship.
9.She was Nominated for universal festival.
Star India award for educational work.
10.Received womens day award.
11.She was the part of anthology Petals 2020
12.Was also a part of anthology khawabo ka silsala and more than 100 anthologies
13.She published a quote book under Your quote 'Mere Sabd Meri Jindagi'
14.She received more than 1000 participation and appreciation certificate.
And many more….

   She has successfully made a video for the students for a tough topic like Schizophrenia.As
Schizophrenia is a chronic and severe mental disorder that affects how a person thinks, feels, and behaves. People with schizophrenia may seem like they have lost touch with reality. Although schizophrenia is not as common as other mental disorders, the symptoms can be very disabling.
 She's loves Anchoring , She reads multiple books, She Writes Poems and Acts, Performs in Drama, Writing shayari Etc
She's fluent in Hindi, English, Marathi Arabic reading
Her Favourite Authors are William Shakespear, Munshi Premchand (Hindi)
Her Favourite poetry : Robert Frost, Harivanshrai bacchan
Her Favourite Books : Tempest and As You like It written by William Shakespear , Godan written by Munshi Premchand.

Pain To Fame

It was a journey of princess
With lot of fences
She was calm and quiet
Respectable and polite

She at the age of three
Was not at all free
She was not allowed to play
Her activities delay

She never knew the truth
She never knew the bitter fruit
But she never ever blame
She always was same

As she was teen
There were lot of scene
People tried to stop her college
So that she can be departed from knowledge.

She was having one lifeline
Which she believes will shine
He was his support
He was her learning passport

He was his no other
But her own father
She completed her post graduation
With lot of graduation.

Now she took the responsibility
That was of her peoples hospitality

She started working at the age of thirteen
As now her responsibility were keen.

She became a teacher
Slowly became co author
Then she compiler
And then a project coordinator.

In her journey still pain exist
As it became part of gist
She started achieving
She started pursuing

She bagged lot of trophy
With lot of learning of psychology
She became district achiever
And then state achiever

Her father was proud
As every newspaper were having her sound
Then she reached at national
And was always at her level

Her life started adapting
The fact of achieving
Now all her pain
Has turned up to fame...

Now all her pain
Has turned up to fame...

Jagriti Pramanik

She is a teacher by profession. She loves to engage herself in writing out her imagination. She believes in simple living and high thinking. She loves to read and write often. She is fond of nature's company.

<u>Her Race With 'Identity'...</u>

She was in a quest of attention
All through her life but received only rejection
When she was a child she searched for love from her teachers
But back then the kids with sharp minds got the affection
from the mentors
She searched for fame in the threshold of college life
But she remained tangled in the game of friendships in her
life
She found a great companion
Without her she felt like to be in a dungeon
She searched for success on the arena of her career
She indeed got it but again in the form of torch bearer
She looked for respect in her workplace
But she bestowed with duties with no appreciation
Those were the moments when she felt for the need of
recognition.
Keeping everything beside, she now stepped into a new
phase of her life
A beautiful and ever joyous phase, yes now she was in love
Completely engrossed in a very special, beautiful bond
She could feel herself flying 24 /7 in cloud 9
Coz everything with her right now was going fine
Every tale seemed real to her with its incredible fantasies
All in her starry nights with coolest breeze she was
surrounded of pansies
That adorable phase made her look even more pretty and
happy
How unfortunate of her it was to be his love
He was her love, life and the only truth she believed in
But she was only his admiration, who was left to find her
own recognition.

<u>The Grass Is Always Greener The Other Side</u>

It was a clement weather of one fine midsummerevening, he stood motionless and expressionless lost in his solitude sipping on his favourite beverage; black coffee. There was no trace of relief on his face on those sips of coffee he took because it was as cold and bitter as himself. The pleasant and gentle breeze kept blowing leaving him tranquil. The ether was serene but his inner selfwasn't. He was gazing constantly at the exquisiteness he was surrounded by. Standing amid the valleys, soul of the forest with its babbling and burbling streams travelling from its bed towards a perennial destiny he dived into his beautiful yet aching past.

It all started from his childhood when he was in his high school. He was running out of school during the dispersal time and he felt a sudden jerkand the next moment he was on the ground. He lifted his head up and saw her crying like a baby as she too fell down and they had actually bumped.

He quickly got up and extended his hand to help her get up and said, 'I am so sorry, I didn't see you coming'. She turned her head and said, 'Its ok', and stood up with his help dusting herself. While he took few steps to go, 'Really!!! So convenient, you pushed me down and simply saying sorry and going?, she said. 'That's the reason, I said sorry' he replied. She furiously replied, 'Oh, really!!! You think you did a favour on me? Absolutely not. In fact you should even do sit ups for it'. 'What!! Are you serious? Are you crazy, do you think it was all my fault? You should have been careful while getting down of your car? But look at you, you are blaming me for a fault for which we both are responsible,' he said and turned back to move to his house. She thumped her feet and went to Principal's room. She came from Manali and was now getting admission in this new school in Kinnaur in the same state of Himachal Pradesh as her father got transferred in his job. She

joined the school almost towards the end of the session in September. On the next day, the school began as usual with morning assembly. In the assembly they bumped each other again, looked at each other's eyes for a while and those few seconds were enough to remind them where have they met and then immediately turned their faces. The gesture was enough to prove that they reminded of their meet the previous day. After the assembly the students went back to their respective classes. He was sitting on his bench busy taking out his book. Suddenly the teacher entered the class and they all greeted her. 'She is the new student of our school and your class, Raina Malhotra,' the teacher said. She continued, 'She has come from Day Star School Manali. She will continue her high school from here on.' He didn't pay much attention to it. Being the head boy of the class the teacher called him, 'Ryansh, introduce her to the classmates and help her in completing the notes for exam'. 'Yes ma'am,' he replied coldly. But she had frowns on her face as she reminded of the incident the previous day. The teacher left the class. She then searched for a vacant seat very soon occupied it without knowing the fact that she just sat beside him. After some time he too went and sat on his place. She looked at him surprisingly with her eyes wide open and bit her tongue as she realized it was his seat and this time fault was hers. The start was bitter no doubt but the outcome was definitely not bitter. He then helped her in getting used to the new atmosphere and new system of academics there. While doing so, he somewhere developed feeling for Raina. She too was quite friendly with him. It was that time where students from poor background were abandoned from the '#friends' zone'. He too came from a poor background and so didn't have many friends but he was happy that she was friendly to him despite of belonging to a rich family. Time passed by and they became even more close to each other. The +2 final exams also got over and now they were preparing for higher studies and awaiting their results. They were not

meeting often as it was their holiday time and so he realized his love for her. He confessed to self that he loved her but he still wanted to know about her feeling for him. He thought to meet and propose her. And he decided to do it on his birthday. It was 25th June, the date of transformation in his life. He called her and asked her to meet in the park near her house. Both of them arrived in the park and sat on the bench. He was not financially sound so he thought of making the day special for her with his own efforts. He has saved money and bought a ring which was a simple one not of gold, diamond or platinum but was a junk ring for her. He decorated the stone bench with rose petals and made her sit there. They were sitting on a perfect location as it was a moonlit evening and the moon was complete like a silver plate just behind them as if witnessing and blessing their love. After talking for a while, made her stand and said he had a surprise for her. He blindfolded her and took her few steps ahead and then opened her eyes, she was awestruck looking at the park decorated with flowers and written 'I LOVE YOU' with rose petals on the lush green grass and before she could turn back he knelt right in front of her and extended his hand with the ring and said, 'I love you, Riana, will you be mine?.I love you the way night loves the moon and day loves the sun. I know I don't have anything now but I promise you one day I will get everything right on under your feet whatever you desire even in your dreams.' Everything was perfect; the cool breeze, the moonlit night, the glowing moon and the perfect location and pure confession. But in this perfect ambience something went imperfect. She was dumbfounded and stood still but here the surprise on her face was not a happy rather she was annoyed. She threw away his ring and furiously pushed him back and yelled, 'How dare you propose!! Do you have any idea what are you saying? How could you imagine this happening? It's not a fairy tale where a poor can dream to be with a princess. Did you forget about our status? How could you forget about

your identity? I only treated you as a friend because you had been helping me that's it nothing beyond it?' he kept gazing at her and tears rolled down his cheek reflected the light of moon as if the moon was there to wipe his tears. 'But you were very friendly and caring so I thought you too love me,' he said in his shivering voice. She bluntly replied, 'C'mon every next person who helps me I have to be sweet to that person that does not mean I have to love him. You think any girl should be happy to be with you? Look at the way you live, so boring!! You don't hang out with friends, don't party and don't even spend money on friends!! Oops! How would you? You don't have money to spend! And you say you will keep me happy? You can't even fulfil my needs.' He pleaded, 'Please, dear! Give me a chance to prove myself. I want to make my own identity. I will give you every luxury and comfort but that would be of my hard earned money not of my parents' hard earned money. Dear, don't you trust me even that much? I promise give me five years and I will make enough money to fulfil all your needs but please be by my side and become my strength.' She replied, 'You want me to live with you in misery? My parents fulfil my wishes even before it is told. My friends surprise me with expensive gifts. What have you done for me so far except for giving me notes? You don't deserve to be anyone's love.' She creased his heart in every possible way she could and crushed the flowers under her heels and went. He sat there for hours crying and screaming on his poverty. It was his poverty and lack of identity that lost his love -a pure love. He wept till the moon faded away and the sun started making its way from the clouds. But the entire night he was sure of his aim now. He knew what he wanted from life and it was his 'Fame and wealth-the power to rule the world'. 'Sir, it is cold outside, you may catch cold. Aai and baba are waiting for you at the dinner table,' said Ramesh. There was a sudden shiver in his body and he came out of his flashback. It was now five years later, he owned a bungalow

of his own, where he lives with his parents. He got his sister married to a rich entrepreneur and they are settled abroad. He was smart and handsome right from his schooldays and now his success added attraction to his personality. His popularity and personality has created chaos among the most able spinsters to woo him. But he pays no heed to such issues anymore. Ramesh had been their servant for past two years to take care of the bungalow and his parents too. He is more of family than servant. He has achieved what he promised to self. He was renowned name in the country now, he was one of the riches business tycoon of the nation. His profound personality always made him different from others. And from that day he had been working hard till date, even after reaching the proximity of success and fame. His dedication kept growing even after reaching the apex of fame and amenity as if he is still in pursuit of recognition.

Prachi Mayuresh Kunkalienkar

Prachi Mayuresh Kunkalienkar is a writer by passion .She writes blogs and is an avid reader .She has written many poems and essays as well as letters to editors and won many accolades .She has also translated a Marathi book into English and also writes poems,quotes Marathi/ Hindi and short stories in English .She blogs regularly on instagram handle - https://www.instagram.com/bluebloodedmumbaikar_tales/ and believes she is a true Blue blooded Mumbaikar .She lives in Mumbai and in love with the city .Mumbai is her inspiration and teaching is her profession .She enjoys listening to music,reading,writing,appreciates and loves art and meditates and writes in her journal regularly .

You can reach out to her at -prachi.kunkalienkar@gmail.com Instagram: bluebloodedmumbaikar_tales .A teacher by profession,a writer by passion and an avid reader .She has been writing poems,quotes and short stories since the age of 6 . She believes whether it is writing or living a happy life ,simplicity and love are essential for both .She has worked as a translator and also and writes in English , Hindi and Marathi .She appreciates art (in any form) ,loves travelling,music,nature and food .She believes one needs to upgrade oneself and not only be the best version of themselves but also help others to be a better person , humanity is the best religion.. "Never stop learning" one can learn anything at any age ,if one is keen .

<u>Born To Shine</u>

Tara Sharma seemed restless. She thought she would never make it at the interview .She had made so many errors and the people on the jury had observed it .She was constantly wiping her face with a handkerchief and sipping water when she was waiting in the lobby for the results to be announced . "Shweta ,Ankita ,Tanvi and Rikita ...Please follow me" . A lady with a stern face ,black framed spectacles made her feel as if she were a cat ,if she could have ever transformed into an animal . I am Ms Niloufer ..please come with me . Ms Catherine ,can you please accompany Ms Tara to the Principal's cabin ? said Ms Niloufer as Tara got up from my seat as if i had received some electric shock .

Yes Ma'am said a soft and angelic voice as we proceeded to the principal's cabin .She looked into Tara's eyes and for a moment Tara thought Catherine was a mind reader .Catherine said "You were good .Just a little nervous which was quite visible in your demo lecture .Just breathe and give it your best .Don't think too much .You will be selected .All the best ! ``.These words were music to her ears .The words had an effect on her just like a paracetamol would do to a person having a temperature .Instant relief from all the stress and tension ."Sure ! thank you so much for the kind words " replied Tara with a big smile and some sprinkle of confidence in her gleaming eyes as if she were a finalist selected for a national competition. She walked into the room calm and composed and walked out with a smile and said "Thank You " to the receptionist at the counter . She knew she had done a great job

"Ms Tara ,could you please wait for a minute ?" asked Shanti . Shanti was the principal's personal assistant . "Here you go ,Congratulations ! " Welcome to Pristine School of Drama,Performing Arts and Education ``.Shanti handed over

2 sheets of paper which meant the world to Tara .She had triumphed . Finally all her hardwork had paid off .She had been offered a good compensation and all other benefits and perks ,along with annual holidays and an annual trip with the kids one abroad and two domestic . Tears rolled down her eyes as she saw that her daughter was also granted admission to the school and the principal was going to fund all the school expenses for her daughter ,Sapna .Sapna was a 5 year old little girl whose smile used to lit up the Sharma's residence .Tara's husband was in the army and passed away 3 years ago during the Phulwama attack .Tara had collapsed and Sapna ,who was once a chatterbox had suddenly stopped smiling and seemed withdrawn and in her own world .Only once she had asked her mom " Is Papa never going to come back and stay with us ? Is he angry that I talk a lot and annoy him ?Tell him I will be a good girl ,please ask him to come back home .I miss him ." Tara broke down only to be comforted by her brother and her sister in law who had a long conversation with her and made her understand that she had to stand on her own feet and work for a better future for Sapna .Her sister in law encouraged her to do B.ed for 2 years and told her that till she finishes her B.ed and gets a job ,she would take care of her niece and she didn't have to worry about her little one at all . Tara had been a shy girl and never had friends or ventured out much in her college days and immediately got married to Arun Sharma when she graduated .She was quite young and naive .She never thought much about her future . She often asked Arun " What do you think does the future has in store for us ?" . He said " We have a bright future ,we are born to shine .Your hubby is an army man ,so don't give up ,fight bravely with the difficulties and circumstances and just like your name 'Keep Shining '. " The Sharma's had a daughter ,Sapna and she was the apple of their eyes .Everything was going well till Mr Arun Sharma dies in the Phulwama attacks and their world came crashing down .Everything turned upside down and Tara suddenly had to

grow up and be strong overnight .She was just another pampered little girl who was a new mom to a cute little princess and suddenly this was too much .She was determined to work hard and take charge of her life and make her daughter's future bright . Here she was now ,3 years later proud of herself ,determined to do well for her daughter and herself ,with tears in her eyes for her hubby never got to see this side of her being brave and a fighter but she was sure wherever he was ,he would be happy and proud of her and would have said "You are Born to Shine ,Keep Shining ." She suddenly felt as if she had wings and was soaring as she walked out of the school gate once again smiling and looking forward to a better tomorrow .Today was the day she was reborn .People would now recognise her not only as Mr Arun Sharma's wife but as Tara Arun Sharma .Finally she would have her own identity .

Rutuja Gahukar

Rutuja Gahukar is a student studying in arts field in Mumbai. She loves music n playing musical instruments.

She aspires to be a Writer as she likes expressing her thoughts by writing and motivating others to live life in the correct way. Although she writes short stories, her main area of focus is poetry. She doesn't expect to gain Name And Fame but she has love and sympathy for all sorts of people and this motivates her to write and bring solutions to the problems faced by the society. The message in her stories and poems suggests that if we have faith in God, inner peace and happiness automatically occurs.

<u>Importance Of Recognition</u>

Sitting on a couch with a gloomy head in a dark room, a young girl is crying bitterly. With a grim face and tears running down all over her face, she is wailing. Her head has started to ache and she realises she has to stop crying to feel better. Somehow by controlling herself, she slowly looks at an object kept besides her couch on a stand. It was her yellow sunburst guitar which she played all the time. Staring not even for a minute at it, she bursts into tears all again... But why is she weeping? Did she face love failure? Or did she fail in exam? Or is the reason something else? Let me tell you what's the case. You will be amazed on reading this story as it's different from what most of you are thinking.

Well, let me first introduce you to this "crybaby" as most of you would call her; her name is Jade. But I am glad to say that she is graceful and jolly by nature. Yes, being an optimistic person, her outlook on life is positive and different from most of her peers. She believes in living a simple life than a materialistic one. Moreover, being punctual in even the smallest thing is her attribute. Since childhood Jade has interest in music. Although, She's not a virtuoso she has a melodious voice.

When Jade turned 16, she thought of learning a musical instrument viz. guitar so that she could sing more sweetly with a background music and also could play songs!

Soon, she bought an acoustic guitar and joined a guitar class in her vicinity. The guitar teacher was not so concerned about Jade and she too knew this as he would just teach her once and then didn't even bother whether she is practicing properly or not. Neither did he appreciate her for her efforts she took in learning the instrument. This made her feel she's not a good learner. At times due to discouragement from her teacher and contenders she stopped her practice too. Yet her enthusiasm to

play increased as she learnt new lessons in guitar. After a year, she could hardly play simple songs with extremely bad strumming. She played guitar among friends and family but everytime she felt that she was not a good guitarist. Indeed, she wasn't even an intermediate. Jade only knew open chords and some scales. So she asked sir to help her out in it and he even assured her to teach well, but again, Jade was not given much attention. Eventually, a feeling of being ignored emerged in her. Her optimistic nature was fading away. Yet, she had a strong desire to learn the instrument anyhow. Finally, she decided to quit the class and learn guitar on her own through youTube videos.

She started watching various videos and practiced for many hours throughout the day and sometimes at night too. She was determined towards her goal to play guitar fluently. Her notebook used to be with her most of the time as she used to glance frequently whatever she wrote in it. She was having a speedy progress and comparatively in a few months her hard work brought success to her. She completed the guitar course. Now she could be called a real guitarist. "Finally! I'm done." Taking a long breath she exclaimed.

Jade started sending guitar covers to her friends and closed ones. But no one appreciated her or recognised her efforts. She didn't know why it was happening with her! Still, she continued her hard work and kept sharing her covers.

One day, Jade thought of sending one of her recorded guitar videos to her prior guitar teacher. After sending the video, she was surprised to see her sir's call! She told him happily that she had finally learnt guitar on her own. He congratulated her saying, "Jade, i saw your guitar cover and I really liked the way you played it. Keep it up girl!" After hearing this Jade was in tears. First time someone had appreciated her cover so far. It made her so emotional that she couldn't even complete her sentence saying, "thank you...," as her voice was quavering. Teacher understood her emotions and told: "You have done it

Jade! Finally you can play guitar." Jade had a huge smile on her face with immense delight. She felt optimistic and confident. However, her happiness was going to increase by what sir would say next.

"Jade, I want you to play and record "Our joy eternally" song on guitar as I have planned to make a collage video of you and some other guitarists playing this song so that I can send it to a famous bollywood band group. Your future will get set dear if they select you in their band."

She couldn't believe what she had heard. She exclaimed, "Really sir!" At this sir answered affirmatively. Jade certainly said yes for the golden opportunity and also thanked sir for giving her that chance. Jade didn't want to miss it anyhow as her future could change just by recording a cover. She told it to her parents and they were proud of their beloved daughter.

Without wasting even a day she started practicing the song and put her whole mind and soul into it. She was so focused on practicing, that her sleeping hours decreased to 4-5 hours a day. She was conscious not to make even a single mistake. After 3 days of continuous hard work she recorded her guitar cover on "Our joy eternally" and sent it to the teacher.

She curiously waited for sir to watch the video. He watched it in a couple of minutes but instead of appreciating her efforts, he pointed out many mistakes. Jade was suprised as she played the correct chords and there was no problem with the strumming pattern too, it was properly on beat of the song. She showed her cover to her parents and one of her guitarist friends to ensure her accuracy in playing, they too found no mistake. Yet, she asked sir to teach her the correct way to play the song and he agreed to teach her too. And this time she did just as he had taught her and recorded the whole cover again without any mistake which is ideally a tough job. After sending the cover for the second time, her teacher said nothing on the video. She called him to confirm whether she played correctly. Though he said yes but it was not wholehearted.

Jade even after finishing the recording work was dejected. She asked herself, "Why nobody recognises my efforts?"

Days passed but sir didn't send any collage video to Jade. Impatiently, she had to contact him again. After picking up her call he told her that the collage video has been sent to the bollywood band group and that he will be streaming the video on zoom with all the participants.

Jade joined the zoom meeting quite earlier and waited for all the participants to join. Soon the video was displayed. Jade was eager to see herself in it and so, she started to stare at it to find herself. Half of the video ended but Jade didn't lose hope. She was confident that she will be there in the video.

The whole video ended but surprisingly Jade wasn't there in it. She couldn't believe this. Her heart sank. She left the zoom meeting and cried bitterly. "Why!... Why does this happen to me everytime!, " she exclaimed. She felt her efforts went in vain as her participation in the video were as if everything for her. Her future was dependent on it. She was so distressed that she didn't even want to talk to her parents. Her parents became tensed and angrily they called her teacher. They scolded him for his treacherous behavior. He couldn't explain the reason for not taking Jade's cover in the collage video. Finally he asked for forgiveness from Jade...

Jade had missed the golden oportunity. But more than that she lost her optimistic outlook towards herself. She started viewing herself as dumb and useless. She even stopped playing guitar as no one cared for her efforts. Recognition was the only thing she lacked. Just a small complement could encourage her up to focus and be determined no matter what.

Every person in this world needs recognition at some point in his life. That helps him to view himself rationally and be steadfast in everything. Moreover, it gives encouragement. If a company's boss observes his employees' efforts and complements them, they get encouraged and work harder for the welfare of the company. A small baby when

simultaneously starts walking and after a few walks falls down, we never discourage it by saying that the baby fell down! Instead we keep appreciating the baby and as a result, it learns to walk.

Appreciation can make a day, even change a life. A person who is recognised will always do more than what is expected. And it increases the confidence level too. In the case of Jade, her confidence was getting lower and lower. That led her to immense depression. However, now she has come up from it and has decided even if no one recognises her, she will never stop doing things she like, she has taken an oath to be determined and steadfast. Now she has her own musical instrument showroom and teaches Guitar and other instruments along with singing. Also she appreciates her students' efforts and help them to learn music effectively.

Hence, if you too don't receive recognition from others , don't lose hope. Don't work for recognition, do things for your own satisfaction and I assure you that one day, you too will recieve recognition.

Vaishni Venkatesh

Vaishni Venkatesh is Senior Executive – Corporate Sales at Naukri a strong sub-brand of Info edge India. Born and brought up in Chennai. She is a witty marketer, Electronic and Instrumentation engineer by profession completed her BE & MBA (Marketing & HR) from Jeppiaar Engineering College & St. Joseph's College of Engineering. She has also completed her Diploma in Digital marketing.

She received Vajra World Record for her unique book "Senescence of Woman". She has compiled 15+ anthologies and been a co-author for 30+ anthologies. She has published 10+ research papers in international conferences. She is a motivational speaker who is ambitious and charismatic. She has been a resource person and guest speaker for many events, seminars, open mics, and also the MC of several events. She

has grown out to be reckoned with confidence and liveliness personified on stage.

She is curious in nature with a high eagerness to learn new things. She believes that kindness will conquer the world. She draws a solution for every problem beautifully on her wrist. She loves to write because she reach people through her writing, aiming to be a changemaker. She enjoys sharing knowledge and guiding everyone towards their goals. She contributes her active participation in volunteering and social service. She is a person who believes that ultimate purpose of life is not achieving only one's goal but to help the needy as much as possible.

She is an author, orator, compiler, epigrammatist, and artist. She is passionate about research, digital marketing, doodling, new language learning, writing books, compiling anthologies & being co-author in anthologies as well. She is also experienced in event management and event organizing. She aims to be an entrepreneur who can serve the nation by developing students' talents and guiding them in the right path. She has her own food blog with mouth-watering recipes, and reviews named LAFOODBINGE.

Instagram ID: vaishni_venkatesh

LIFE & PAIN

When I was younger, I was a cheerful child who longed for lifelike those fantasies. I longed for a world. A world which my current world precisely didn't end up being. Here and there that would make me dismal that I had no true friend, scarcely not a Single friend who had the option to understand me. Sometimes my heart felt heavier than myself where I cry continuously for hours. The cry may be because of some silly reason like marks or it may be because of the insults I faced because of my relatives and friends. But the show must go on, my life must move on. It cannot pause just for these evil ones.

I just made my mind that I am been tested by God about my patience level and my love towards reaching my goal without any support. But though I wonder why me? Why me among those people who don't even know how to treat people? Is it because of Karma, punishment of my previous life's sins? Here is what I wished I would know sooner, however it hurts more, the more I hold it in. My life was lowered in the water. Water has consistently been my adversary. The individual who turned my life into hellfire. I suffocated in tears, I cried resoundingly in my room, for what reason am I committing such countless errors? For what reason am I not awesome? For what reason is my life so muddled? Why God made me? Tears were my lone sidekick. The torment was my dearest companion and always mine. Tears fell when nothing turns out well for me. Heart ached when I was perfectly imperfect. A moment of introspection all it takes. Pain became an organ within me, which I cannot live apart.

My life was not a walk in the park but rather a bed of thistles. People used to treat me as if I am an abandoned child, they never value my presence. They thought me as a person who cannot be loved and cared for. All I had was a lot of question and my mom who was my pillar of support. Though I was not a bright student in my schooling, I tried to mould myself by utilising each and every opportunities even if it is the most smallest opportunity

which can be provided. I gave myself a chance to move forward and to begin again.

My primary aphorism was to acquire insight, get placed in a decent organization and, make myself monetarily autonomous. Life changed completely when I started to concentrate on my studies. I became the most brightest student in my college. I started my writing career by writing as a co-author, gradually turning myself into a compiler and finally I was able to launch my solo book "Senescence of Woman" on women's day by explaining the different phases of life of a women. And who knew that my first solo book will be recognized for Vajra World Record for its unique topic.

After facing continuous pain in my life, all I had was belief in God and belief in my mother's blessing which turned my life to complete fame. I am now a motivational speaker who motivate students and guide them towards their destiny. And I also have my own food blog. I also became an successful entrepreneur by starting my own Digital event management start up and publication. I became a multitasker by being all that I wished to be. I still did not pause my dreams and goals, and still have my bucket list which is trembling with dreams and goals. All what I believed is though God has taken most valuable things from my life and has gifted me sorrow throughout my life, the more I endure pain the more I succeed and walk towards the path of fame.

Urge yourself to taste achievement and distinction. Make an existence where you can never be judged. Once you are done crying, just look at those precious tears which helped you to endure the pain you underwent with. Wipe those tears off because those tears are the symbol of the pain of your past. Though these tears are not magical spells which can cause miracles but trust me they can make wonders. This phase of life, this pain will also pass, and tomorrow will be a day which will make your fame last forever. Its not a poem, it's a part of my life's art and I am always ready to restart.

Zala Ramiben Devsibhai

She is Zala Ramiben from Veraval ,Gir Somnath.She publish her write up with Nick name Sandeshi.She got many award in literature.She got second rank in state level letter writing contest.She got three certificate of vajra world record and two certificate from book of india world record and a certificate from OMG world record.Her four solo book published.She being part of 75 anthology.She also complie three anthology.

अनुभूति

बहोत आसान सा है संबंध बनाना।
इतना ही कठीन है अनुभूतियां के साथ उसे निभाना।।
सिर्फ नाम के रह जाते है कई संबंध।
फिर वो बन जाता है एक बड़ा बंधन।।
हो अगर अनुभूति एवम प्यार सामने वाले पात्र से।
जीवन धन्य बनता है दोनो का इस अनुभूति से।।
कई कठीन मार्ग बन सकते है सरल।
जीवन बन जाता है तरल।।
हो अगर अनुभूति एकदूजे के लिए।
दिया जाए साथ जीवनभर के लिए।।
होता है आसानी से सामना कठीन परिस्थिति का।
यही तो है महत्व संबंध में अनुभूतियों का।।
चाहे वो माता पुत्र हो या सास बहू।
चाहे वो बाप बेटा हो या पति पत्नी।।
चाहे गुरु शिष्य हो,चाहे हो कोई पड़ोसी।
जरूरत से नही जुड़े अनुभूतियां से।।
दो हस्त फैलाकर कर रही अरज संदेशी।
बनाओ अगर संबंध तो दिलोजान से निभाओ।।
न निभा सके अनुभूति के साथ ।
बनाओ ही न किसी से संबंध आप।।

शॉर्ट एवम स्वीट

अगर प्यार की न हो अनुभूति दिल में ।
थकान एवम कड़वाहट आएगी संबंध में।।

अगर न हो अनुभूति दिल में।
लगे थकान थोड़े से कार्य में।।

हो अगर अनुभूति किसी के लिए।
बिना थकान सारा दिन काम हो जाए।।

अनुभूति ही है हमारे जीवन की शान।
जिएंगे अनुभूति के साथ मिलेगा सम्मान।।

Flairs and Glairs, a platform by a student for the students. We are esteemed youth struggling to carve out our path for our future and we follow a basic mindset Since everyone is not born with all-round skills. Joining hands with people who are born to execute it with perfection is the best way to evolve. Self-Evolution is the need of the hour but, evolving as a community is what we strive for. The initiative as kickstarted by, Founder- Mr. Shubham Shah with the motive to utilize the skillset and talent of writing has now a team of 10+ people who are actively participating into newer forms of learning and discovering talents among youngsters. We Provide platform and services like Publishing opportunities, Open mics, Workshops, Hands-on training. Operating with Brand Name of Flairs and Glairs (Publication House), we offer the chance of elevating a passionate writer to an esteemed author With Brand name Teekhe Zasbaaat. We bring to you an opportunity to get accustomed with the Public Speaking and Presenting of Thoughts along with regular challenges to brush up your inking spirit. The newest initiative to extend our services we introduced in a new writing Platform- The Glittering Fables and Ink Over Tears.

We Choose to Fly Like A Falcon than to be

a Leg Pulling Crab.

To Know More: Infoline – 7781900870

Mail Us At-

flairsandglairs@gmail.com / info@flairsandglairs.in

Or Visit is at

www.flairsandglairs.com / www.flairsandglairs.in

Social Handles- @flairsandglairs @teekhezasbaaat

www.ingramcontent.com/pod-product-compliance
Lightning Source LLC
LaVergne TN
LVHW021244200726
843509LV00012B/1587

9789390799862